Paper Boats

sailing through the waves and tides of life

Neoniel Pedutem

Ukiyoto Publishing

All global publishing rights are held by

Ukiyoto Publishing

Published in 2024

Content Copyright © Neoniel Pedutem

ISBN 9789360494858

*All rights reserved.
No part of this publication may be reproduced, transmitted, or stored in a retrieval system, in any form by any means, electronic, mechanical, photocopying, recording or otherwise, without the prior permission of the publisher.*

The moral rights of the author have been asserted.

This book is sold subject to the condition that it shall not by way of trade or otherwise, be lent, resold, hired out or otherwise circulated, without the publisher's prior consent, in any form of binding or cover other than that in which it is published.

www.ukiyoto.com

Dedication

To my family, friends, Rose Antonette (my daughter by heart), Icy (my girlfriend), and to all the valiant sailors who are braving the waves and tides of life.

Contents

Prose 1

under the plumeria tree 2
a mano 4
a letter to myself 6

Poetry 8

yuletide season 9
hopeless. 10
the secret masterpiece 11
winter love 13
a writer's case 15
the empyrean 17
this pain 18
just only your name 19
great love 21
april fool's day 22
saturdays 23
memories 25
the plight of moving on 26
lato-lato fever 27
the things I love 28
the love I know 30
someday, somewhere 31
how? 33
the little universe 35
no more sad poems 36
august 37
not too much 39
my yellow 40
bounce 41
toad 42
golden 43

earthworm	44
naked & whole	45
of being a star	46
childhood	48
never-never land	49
a letter to sadness	50
the future without you	51
who's next?	53
this is me trying	55
sail away	57
river	59
just be you	61
imagine	63
footnote	64
wishful thinking	65
logophile	66
empathy	68
love is not enough	70
blue christmas	71
just maybe	72
About the Author	73

Prose

under the plumeria tree

May 5, 2023, Friday. The weather was so kind; the sunlight unclothed the stitches of my scars and the air lifted my weight. I was wearing well-ironed plain white t-shirt and black ankle-length trousers. I sprayed a generous amount of perfume – a mild and laid-back type of scent. Courage was my only priceless accessory.

There were strips of old films playing inside my head while I was inside the car.

Five years ago, I met a girl whom I was in the lavender haze with. She promised me that I was the man she was dreaming for. I held on to that, it stayed with me. We ate breakfast together at a famous fast-food chain on her birthday. The conversation started with sheer silence. I threw some compelling jokes but she was still downright blank, preoccupied. Perhaps, I ruffled her feathers for being too annoying. I almost finished eating when she said, "I'm breaking up with you."

She left without any reason. After two weeks, I saw her holding another man's hand while she was crossing the street. Her face was so light and lovely.

I just walked away and shrugged my shoulders. After all, I became part of her. I wanted her to be happy even if that happiness no longer includes me.

I travelled to South for two hours. The town was so welcoming, I felt I was an invited guest walking on a red carpet. Getting closer to where she was working at trembled my knees. Rubbing both of my palms against each other helped me feel less nervous somehow. I kept walking back and forth while rehearsing how to greet her in a most respectful way.

At lunch time, she went downstairs and I easily noticed her long wind-swept hair with burgundy ribbon hair clip. I saw in my peripheral view her colleagues who were suppressing their giddyness and evident excitement. Seconds after I greeted her, we went straight to a beach resort which is famous for its picturesque view and placidness.

Everything was so slow, spontaneous, and natural. The enthralling seawater, the azure sky, and the abundance of flowers contrived sublimely together for our first meeting. I handed a short note to her while waiting for our order. It was quite awkward. But the conversation was getting more serious when I held her hand, and I recited how clear my intention was in pursuing her.

She nodded. I paused and looked at her amber eyes. That very moment, I felt I was doing the right thing. And it was pure and beautiful.

We went for a short walk at the vineyard. She delightfully told me how charming my smile was. I just put my right hand in my pocket because my heart was frantically pounding.

There, under the plumeria tree, our invisible strings began to attach and I hoped fate will favor us forever.

a mano

The half of my body was leaning against the quilted headboard, bewildered by how the government finds panacea for the traffic conjestion in Manila. I was here 11 years ago during my freshman year in college and I knew that there were still skeletons in the closet.

Fear robbed my voice when I was a young adult, so I never had the chance to speak my truth. I slept in silence, powerless. Why most adults associate talking back with disrespect? Why they impose the idea that they're always right? I just cried and only my tears understood the weight of my pain. As much as I wanted to release the throbbing squash, I kept them in me and nursed them with the cradle of time.

Someone silently knocked at the door. It was Aya, my first cousin (father side). She asked me to go for a walk in Bonifacio Global City. However, I was bone-tired after I attended an international event for accomplished people. I heard the sigh of her desperation. The short hand of the clock almost hit seven, so I took a quick cold shower and left the house.

The city lights were dancing around my irises. I was astonished by multitude of people when we arrived at the midpoint. My cousin shared her go-to places: the famous restaurants, clubs, clothing stores, and homey coffeeshops. Then, she directed me to well-known photo spots apt for instagram feed.

After strolling for few minutes, we stopped by *a mano*, an Italian restaurant located in the long stretch of stores at BGC. We ordered two glasses of aperol sangria with burnt orange peel. I was not a cocktail aficionado but I knew that more than its bittersweet taste, something would be revealed over the table.

I wasn't wrong or maybe my clairvoyant eye was finally unveiled. After few sips, my cousin shared a strip of her inner struggle growing up. Looking at her, it seemed that she was raised from an almost perfect household. Sadly, I was a victim of visual deception— that what we see in the faces of people is just a mere speck of them.

She was so honest, an instant storyteller for two hours. I understood the language of her sighs. I read the rough lines in between of her pauses. Never that I imagined that I rekindled my soul with her after 11 long years.

The skeletons in the closet grew flesh and they came to life eventually. I was just kind enough to listen, and that made a difference.

a letter to myself

Dear Neyo,

Hey! It has been a rough year for you. Time has finally revealed how much you can only catch and release at the same time. You can't carry it all at once. The weight will just slowly rot your bones and turn them into dust if you try to hold them whole. Making it light seemed like bathing in the river of hell.

Some people would steal a piece of your narrative and make you as antagonist. They might discredit all your help especially on the things that you wholeheartedly gave without them asking. They might see you as rusting mechanical parts of a watch if you're no longer vauable to them. Unfortunately, your heart of gold still shines for them no matter how poor they treat you. They still occupy the little spaces in your life despite them closing their doors for you.

You have so much love to give. You're always there for them even if it demands much of your time and it costs you inconvenience. Still and all, you feel not enough. You easily give things that you wish you also receive. Sadly, when you need them at the rarest time, they have a lot of excuses. Oftentimes, they make you feel that they are out of reach.

As you keep walking on the path you are not certain where it leads you, stay faithful to the campass that you are holding. God will direct your feet to the place you rightfully belong.

Do not wait for someone to be a hero for you. Not everyone has the same heart as yours. If you can use your power to save others, you can do it on yourself more.

Keep sailing, Neyo!

Poetry

yuletide season

I believe in the use of
evergreen embellished with
turtle doves, ribbons, and pinecones
as a symbol of permanence.

May the carols of December
give them life and sing
in the tune of hallelujahs,

rejoice with the
angels in chorus,

play with the pitter-patter of
little silver bells, and

rekindle the spirit
caged for a long time.

I believe that anyone can be
a string of light that wraps
the skin of the
                hopeless.

the secret masterpiece

if you could be a painting,
you are a sunset — a sky's
masterpiece, a fleeting
scarlet and violet.

the night always steals
your ravishing beauty
as you gloriously display the
colors in a borderless canvass.

you are the language
of silence that my heart
easily understands.

so, if you could be a painting,
I would love to hang you on
my alabaster bedroom wall,

always close to my eyes
always close to my heart,

something that you don't know.

winter love

the moonstone of your heart
and the frostbite of winter
have no difference at all.

you left me at the graveyard,
buried me without remorse
on a deserted land
covered with a heap of
fractals and snowflakes.

I slowly died in a snowstorm
while reaching for the
warmth of your touch, but

you walked away
indifferently with no
traces of footprints.

you are the ache of my December —

the saddest month of the year
that I will always remember.

a writer's case

to me, unable to write
for long time is a crime.

a drop of pen
handcuffs both of
my worn-out hands.

the crumpled sheets of
paper scattered on
the floor demand
an apology.

I always try to
ran away like a fugitive
but my conscience
patrols everywhere.

so, I keep coming back
and be a slave of words.

for in writing,
I am **f r e e**.

the empyrean

I can't carry it all at once.

I am only a fine dust
amalgamated into a big entity.

There are some things
I have to hold, and
there are some things
I have to let go, so

when I step on acrid smolder,
barefooted, wandering the unknown
places until I go back to dust,

I am light enough
to reach the heaven's gate

and hold the most powerful hand.

this pain

I really know this pain —
of being held up in the sky,
marvel how each cloud arrays
a heavenly architecture, then
drop me forthwith in the fires of hell.

I know exactly how this pain
sleeps in my bones for ages,
how the thin fibers of my flesh
cower in fear for another promise.

I know how this pain
grows thorns in my chest,

but this pain helped me discover

how much love I can give and
how much I am willing to lose.

just only your name

It is always in the afterglow
of vermillion sky that I remember
the last letter I gave to you,
sealed with a scarlet wax.

I wonder if you read it.

Each word was engraved
on a lonely sheet,
soaked in dry poignant tears.

It has no intention on holding you back,
and stay in the cradle of my arms, but
I want you to know how happy I was
when we painted the whole town red
in summer and how we danced
under the hovering fireflies

I thought it won't last.
If I see that picturesque display again,
I hope I could only remember your name.

great love

I always wonder what great love is.

Is it the morning cuddles — wrapping around someone's skin, the warmth seeping through the dwelling of flesh and bones?

Is it the offering of time to a yearning soul

despite the treachery of a clockwork

as an immortal Nemesis?

Is it giving your all — from the little quiver of your heartbeat to the falling of your moonstone tears?

Is it growing old together, talking about

the highschool romance while lying on the rocking chairs in the late afternoon together?

I keep wondering, not until

I saw a great Man who died on the cross.

april fool's day

You're the saint of April Fool's Day
everyone does not know about.
You love to be praised by many
but you suddenly hate the clout.

The deception of your warm touches
commands my heart to obey the lies.
Dishonesty is your casual card game,
you keep the truth by playing nice.

If you try to trick me again by words
similar to a sad tragic movie line,
put them in your empty shallow pockets
because I am now perfectly fine.

saturdays

all Saturdays should always
be gentle and slow.

in every stretch
of the worn-out limbs
is an unpopular work
of art on a mattress.

after the last sip
of a morning coffee
the heart remains calm —
unbothered of the tumultuous
noise marching anywhere.

the time keeps on running,
but there is no chasing
of mocking deadlines anymore,
no deep-seated guilt for doing nothing,
for Saturday is only for us,

a temporary escape
from the tortures of life.

memories

oftentimes, a reel of memories
plays during silence.

it would flash sad episodes at the ceiling
that your eyes don't want to see anymore,
the walls display your favorite scenes
that would evoke the moments you wish to stay,

and

the floors seem to gather all your tears
after nights of self-inflicted lamentations.

your mind becomes a cinema that offers
free tickets and shows you the reality
on the big screen which you hardly believe.

it is always in the film of silence that
your heart remembers what your mind avoids.

the plight of moving on

we can move on
but the moments
sealed in a memory
are ardently nourished
by immortality.

it does not cater death,
it only enjoys its dormancy
and appear again without a warning
on a big screen of our little heads,

and it shows;

the mind replays what
the heart can't delete.

lato-lato fever

the series of clacking sound
follows me anywhere
as if my poor eardrums
become a docile minion of it.

out of curiosity,
I hold a grip on it
and I understand how
hard it is to master
the play.

then, I ask myself:

why some people
hate to see
the happiness
of others?

the things I love

I have my own list
of the things I love:

I love to photograph
the early morning dews
that slowly glides through
the leaves.

I love to sip a cup
of coffee in silence
and remember how
our clandestine romance
ended in September.

I love to read a book
on a somber weather,
be a slave of the author
from prologue until I dissociate
from the last page, and

I love the uncertain —
of being so unsure
if the love that I give
will be requited
the same way.

the love I know

I want to carry the meaning of love,
not to be a miserable victim of it.

The kind of love that is not perfect
but it is defined by all the gentleness —
in words, in actions, in thoughts

It is also a record of good and bad
memories in a running clock
that perseveres to smoothen the rust
and hopes to stay in the light
despite its absence.

Love shouldn't be a criminal:
a murderer of faithfulness,
a robber of trust,

and if it happens,
I would be scared
to *begin again*.

someday, somewhere

s o m e d a y
s o m e w h e r e
you will sail away
from the scathing claws
and raucous hubbub
of the wrathful ground.

you will disengage the anchor
from a long-lived halt and
begin another grand voyage —
patch a thousand cuts,
move on without revenge,
and shower yourself
with kindness again.

no apology can heal
the open wounds,
so, bury the forgiveness
on the seabed and

write nothing on
the tombstone.

someday you will sail away,
far enough that no one can reach

somewhere you rightfully belong.

how?

how to unsee
the fine lines
of your face
that are heaven
to my irises?

how to forget
the late-night chats,
the coffee dates,
and the karaoke sessions
if you are the only memory
my heart remembers?

how to let go
from the comfort
of your hands
if you have been
my safe place
for a long time?

how to unlearn
to love you
if I still believe
in your lies?

the little universe

I grow up standing on a pinnacle
by giving birth to constellation of stars.
People see how they shine at me,
bright enough to cover all my scars.

I dream for a bigger universe
with billions of galaxies that I don't know.
The more I desperately aspire for it,
the more asteriods and blackholes grow.

I steal the crown of Saturn,
I rob the beauty of the moon.
The sun wonders my whereabouts
as if I consider it as a supreme boon.

I become a thief of others' dreams,
floating into the nebula of selfishness. Occupying all the spaces in the universe
won't give me the kingdom of greatness.

no more sad poems

I don't want to write sad poems anymore: **Betrayal. Grief. Misfortune. Death. Misery**

I want to write the theatrical display
of sunset soaked in scarlet and amethyst,
the dulcet interlude of crickets in summer,
the strangers crossing the urban street, and
the abundance of plumerias in May.

I often encounter them,
but my memory seems a bygone joy —
of the mundanity and ordinary.

Sad poems are now in the burrow.

They have lived long enough, adieu.

august

If I only knew how fast
the passing of August,
I would write the name
of grief on a gravestone,
and the epitaph is:

"Living is painful. Death does not feel hurt."

I would bury myself thirteen feet,

let the earth slowly consume my flesh and bones. The decaying white chrysanthemums strew, the candles muster light.

There, under,
I would only hear
the echoes of familiar footsteps
while I quaff a bottle of tequila
until I weep no more, so
when September comes,
I am strong enough

to recite another elegy

for myself...
                        again.

not too much

I don't ask for too much.

Just hold my hand and own
the little spaces of my fingers,
take them to a place where your heart
only knows the pulchritude of my name.

That each step of our feet
follows the unplanned destination
and the collected dusts as audience
of how the distance gets jealous of us.

Don't make any promises,
I might hold onto them
until they become fragments
of the love I kept in the
chambers of my heart.

I don't ask for too much
but I know I deserve more.

my yellow

She belongs to the home of yellow.
As the sunrays nestle on her face,
It grows plethora of wild sunflowers.
The night cannot dim its refulgence,
Even the menace of the nimbus clouds.
She is a bearer of fire:
A warmth for grieving souls,
A relief for weary bones.
She marches in a parade of gold flakes
Under the blanket of tuscan sky.
Among the colors before my eyes,
She is the definition of the brightest,
                    My *Daylight*.

bounce

I remember five summers ago
when we jumped on a trampoline.
Your rosewood plaid skirt twirled
as the wind began its blowing.

Your plum-scented hair seeped
through the walls of my nose.
I wished it to stay longer than a century
although you treated me like a ghost.

Through all the highs and lows,
I kept holding you as much as I can
but you suddenly bounced back
and fell in love with another man.

toad

I live in an outskirt swamp
where wild lotus and lilies thrive.
The shrubs, the mosses, the pelicans
under the azure sky, we intertwine.

But you disrupt the placidness
by polluting the clarity of the water.
The horns growing on your head
is as long as the size of the river.

I may seem smaller than you
cause I am only a toad that croaks.
But you will gasp for thin air if I clapback
when your own fear slowly chokes.

golden

I used to be your favorite canvass
and drenched me with the rain of yellow.
You let me sip the nectar of a sunflower
as I walked barefooted in the meadow.

Your kiss was as sweet as honey,
 the bees were so jealous about.
My eyes shone like a dazzling amber
that covered the big lies in your mouth.

The frostbite of winter love had begun
before I felt my heart gradually got rotten.
The tint of yellow left in me vanished
when you painted another canvass, *golden*.

earthworm

I would want to be reincarnated
in the life of an earthworm —
no skeletons, only segmented body,
the one that does not know how to mourn.

There is no need to look for a spouse,
build a family and produce an offspring.
As a hermaphrodite, I can do it all alone
so, I don't have to buy a wedding ring.

I would spend most of my life underground slithering
anywhere without a limit
but not knowing where the path leads
is what inspires me to travel it.

naked & whole

there is abundance in my bareness.

the thin fingers of my branches
have nothing to hold anymore
after the autumn's demise.

when the wind does its visitation,
no music plays, poetry holds its tongue
silence screams so loud, reverberating

if I don't pass through this phase —
of being empty, completely naked

I won't appreciate the beauty
of being full again.

of being a star

I am alone outside
so, I whisper to the night
if I can be one of its stars
and collects the wishes
of hopeful dreamers.

I will record
in the cassette tapes
the sorrows in their sighs,
the shortness of their breaths,
the language they can't speak.

I will rewrite
in the blank pages
the anecdotes of their disbelief,
the tales of their debacle,
the footnotes of their doubts.

I will pin on the corkboard

the vignettes of tomorrow
and tell them that I will stay
here tonight and
a billion years more.

childhood

Deym, I'm growing up so fast.

I miss jumping on a haystack,
catching dragonflies in the meadow,
flying paper planes in the backyard,
stealing watermelons in summer,
and playing hide-and-seek at midnight.

I wish my little memory
would bring back my innocence:

when afternoon nap
was still a punishment,
that a handful of candies
could easily mend the pain,
and Christmas was still my favorite holiday.

If I could only revisit my childhood,
I would stay and I won't count
the number of days ever again.

never-never land

take me to kinder place:

where people don't only see
the tip of the iceberg,
the surface of the water
or the cover of an old book,

people who live in gentleness,
just as how the spider tangles
the silken threads of a cobweb
or the oscillation of pampas
when the wind does its dancing.

take me there now
where sadness does not stay,
it only passes like a stream

and when I get there,
I will build a bridge
for everyone to cross over.

a letter to sadness

Hi, sadness!
I know it's you again.
Why do you love to gatecrash
the life of the party in my head?

I just want to dance and scream
on the top of my lungs, orchestrate
my feet away from the conundrum
while I take off the clothes of my scars.

Tonight, I would like to be surrounded
by the string of lights, wrap my skin
with a whiff of vermouth and tequila
to shelter my heart before your arrival.

You are an uninvited guest
my eyes cannot recognize.
If you want to join now,
only for a while — not for too long.
I am happy without you.

the future without you

If we no longer walk
on the same direction
and begin to fall apart,

it is not the memories
that would lay me
on the bed of sorrows
and play a death's game.

It is not in the photographs
where we both chiseled
beautiful curves on our faces.

It is not in our favorite song
that defines the kind of joy
if you put your fingers
in between spaces of my hand.

It is the hope in the future

where I would wait for you
in the altar and take a vow
that won't happen anymore.

who's next?

we crossed the urban street
on the 12th day of November,
we stayed in the coffeeshop
and ordered two iced lattès.

we sat near the big glass window
and watched the footsteps of
the passersby, curious about
the places they were heading to.

I grabbed a napkin and a pen,
composed a poem for her
when the clouds began to mourn.

I secretly put it in the pocket
of her coat hanging on
an empty wooden chair.

that was the last time I saw her

and I wondered who would be
my next muse —

the ache of my poetry.

this is me trying

I go to bed tonight
with a lump in my throat
and shortness of breath

as if the whole universe
takes up the spaces
of my backbones
and resides at my chest.

I disown my strength,
bury it in the darkness
and let it rest in the bosom
of the clockwork for a while.

I surrender my fears,
the clamor of my heart,
and the demise of hope
in the deathbed of time

but the sun will rise
and I will try again.

Trying is already enough.

sail away

I pull up the anchor and
unmoor the rope of the boat.
Plot the map and take the
compass out from my coat.

The voyage begins,
there's a peril waiting on the seafloor.
But I leave all my doubts and misgivings
in the lungs of the shore.

I get along with the waves
and tame them to be still.
How vicious the current is
when its fate is to mercilessly kill.

Braving the crest and trough
is an art I must master.
So, I study thoroughly
the unpredictable rhythm of the water.

As I continue sailing,
the raging storm forms from a distance.
I cower in fear when the sky dims,
I might lose the balance.

If I fall into the deep, I rise again
and swim no matter how far.
I follow the reverberating echo
that leads to where you are.

river

the river flows in you —
oh love so gentle, free,
and persevering.

you are the water
that travels from high ground
to the unfamiliar places
that you will leave behind.

you surrender in the current,
let its strength take you far away,
pass through the curves
and boulders' crevices.

sometimes, you cascade
from unknown heights
and fall into a strife

and there you are,

you reach the sea;

immense,
　　deep,
healing.

just be you

most young people say
they want to be like me

please, **DON'T !**

there are legions
of centaurs and goblins
camping in my chest

my head throws a party
for running chariots
and dauntless gladiators
where they celebrate
in conundrum

I worship greatness
as my god, the one that
could save me
from shame

and the spotlight
is my religion

it is not easy to be me,
so just be you

always and in *all ways*

imagine

imagine a life,

you live in a cottage
in the woods alone,
own the ephemeral
grandeur of sunrise

take a morning walk,
sit by the lake under
the willow and throw
pebbles on the water

when the night comes,
you set up a bonfire
and watch how embers
paint the afterglow
in your irises

just imagine a life —
quiet, slow, and simple

footnote

You can tap your own back if breathing seems an eclipse of moths devouring your lungs. Your hands are meant to comfort yourself first before you do it to others.

wishful thinking

I wish I am still the reason
why you're awake at midnight,
someone who understands
the language of your sighs.

I wish my name is still on your lips.
I wish I still feel the warmth of your kiss.

I wish this love is sublime.
I wish I could still call you mine.

logophile

words;

they decay,
they rot
if you let them
motionless

they run away
like a criminal
and burn
the law

they visit like
autumn air

they disappear
like embers
in a campfire

sometimes,
you let them die
and they're better like that,

lifeless

empathy

Empathy:

I will try to wear
your clothes made
of deep wounds
and livid bruises.

I will try to fit
my feet in your
worn out shoes
and walk them
on the path that
you already took.

I will try to wear
the choking
weight of your
necklace.

I will try to wear
your soul to
understand what
is it like to be you.

love is not enough

oh Dear, love is not
only love alone

it takes courage
by braving the storm,
leaping over the holes,
and defying the odds

it takes hard work
by carrying the loads,
weaving the threads,
and navigating the future

Dear,
love cannot survive
in this world only by
just loving

blue christmas

Silver bells didn't ring
Angels forgot how to sing
Sadness was my present
I wore it as an ornament
Turtle doves failed to fly
Some old nutcrackers cried
Gingerbread grew molds
It was dark in all households
There is nothing left to say
So, I slept on Christmas Day
It could have been fun and merry
If you only made time to greet me

just maybe

maybe, we met early in this lifetime
because we won't grow old together

maybe, our love is a gamble
and I would go home with empty pockets

About the Author

Neoniel Pedutem

Neoniel Pedutem was born and raised in Mina, Iloilo, Philippines. He has a degree in Secondary Education major in English. He is also a local writer, public speaker, badminton enthusiast, and an adviser of a youth organization. His first poetry book, Homebound, was published in December 2022.

www.ingramcontent.com/pod-product-compliance
Lightning Source LLC
LaVergne TN
LVHW041543070526
838199LV00046B/1812